FART SQUAD

FARTASAURUS REX

by **SEAMUS PILGER**

illustrated by **STEPHEN GILPIN**

HARPER

An Imprint of HarperCollins Publishers

full
fathom
five

Out of nowhere, the tar pit bubbled and belched. It filled the air with a sour, stomach-turning smell that stank worse than a porta-potty after a chili cook-off.

But the disgusting smell wasn't the worst thing rising from the pool of sticky black tar. Dozens of school kids on a field trip to the

site stared wide-eyed at the pit. Their jaws dropped and their stomachs turned.

A huge scaly head poked up from the gaseous soup. Prehistoric yellow eyes looked around at the modern world. Slimy drool dripped from hungry jaws. The tip of an enormous tail shot up from beneath the gooey surface of the pit. Bubbles burst from the tar, as if someone had let a giant fart rip in the bath, and a moment later, another disgusting burst of stink polluted the air, causing people to gag, plug their noses, and run for their lives.

FARTASAURUS REX LIVED AGAIN!

CHAPTER ONE

EARLIER:

Darren Stonkadopolis had been looking forward to this field trip for weeks. As a die-hard dinosaur-lover, Darren's favorite place to visit was the Buttzville Prehistoric Tar Pit & Museum. He never got tired of the local tourist attraction. Besides the pit itself, the museum contained fossils of ancient creatures trapped in the gooey tar millions of years ago, a museum, gift shop, and dinosaur-themed cafeteria. But the key piece of the

museum's collection was the rarest of all dinosaurs, the long-extinct "Buttosaurus." It was the only one of its type and scientists believed it may have only ever existed in Buttzville.

"Check out those razor-sharp teeth," Darren said, pointing them out to his best friend, Andy Blackman, as they admired

the colossal skeleton, which towered above them on its hind legs outside the museum. Rows of sawlike fangs lined the dinosaur's bony jaws. "That's how you know it was a meat-eater. A predator!"

Andy probably already knew that, Darren figured. His friend was one of the brainiest kids at Buttzville Elementary School, after all. But Darren couldn't resist raving about the skeleton and dinosaurs in general. They were just too cool to keep quiet about.

"Boy, wouldn't you like to see one of these in real life!"

Andy peered at the scary-looking skull through a thick pair of glasses. The tar had stained the bones a dark brown color. "Actually, I think I like keeping one hundred fifty million years between us."

While the entire fourth grade explored the paved pathways around the tar pit, the teacher in charge, Miss Priscilly, tried to keep all the children under control. She only had Stan, the school janitor, to help. He had come along as an extra chaperone. The hardest kid to mind was also the richest—Harry Buttz Jr. The school and the town were named after his father. They still owned half of Buttzville. That's why Harry felt he could ignore the safety rail surrounding the pit and go in to get a closer look.

"Unhand me!" Harry squealed, when Stan grabbed him by the shirt to save him from falling in. "I'll have your job!" he yelled as he tugged at his collar.

"Children, children!" Miss Priscilly called out. "Gather round and pay attention while our host, Professor Paleo, kindly explains the educational value of this site."

The museum curator had been conducting

the Tar Pit tour ever since Darren was a little kid. He was a good friend of Darren's. Frizzy white hair escaped from under the pith helmet he wore. Professor Paleo winked at Darren before launching into his lecture, which Darren practically knew by heart:

"Millions of years ago, a prehistoric swamp existed where Buttzville now is. Liquid tar seeped up from the earth and created a deceptively deep pool. Dinosaurs and other primitive animals would wander over and some were unlucky enough to fall in it. Unlucky for them, but lucky for us. Their fossils were preserved in the pit when the tar hardened into thick, solid sludge. We've extracted many fossils from

this site, such as that Buttosaurus skeleton on display over there. It is one of an entire genus of large-butted, vicious flesh-eating dinosaurs. Nobody knows how deep the pit goes, or what else might be trapped down there, preserved forever by the tar. . . ."

Darren's mind wandered, imagining the ancient swamp and its spectacular wildlife. All the excitement and activity had given him an appetite. Throughout the tour, Darren had been munching on nuts and pretzels that he'd bought from a vending machine. But the salty snacks had made him super thirsty. When he tried to slip off to the water fountain, Ms. Priscilly stopped him in his tracks. "No leaving the class!" Darren tried to explain, but Ms. Priscilly was clearly down to her last nerve.

"Pssst," he whispered to Andy. "I'm dying here. You got anything to drink?"

"What happened to your water bottle?" Andy whispered back.

squirt

"I drank it all already." Darren licked his lips, but his mouth felt as dry as the fossilized bones. "Guess I should've saved some for later."

"I've got half a root beer left." Andy fished a plastic soda bottle out of his backpack. "It's mostly backwash, but help yourself."

Root beer?

Darren eyed the bottle nervously. Ever since he'd eaten those radioactive burritos a few weeks ago, his digestive system had been touchy—to say the least. The burritos had given him and his friends Tina, Walter, and Juan-Carlos super fart powers that they were only just learning to control. His gassy insides hadn't acted up in a while, but he'd been especially careful to steer clear of sodas just to be safe. Maybe a root beer wasn't such a good idea, especially after the bumpy bus ride.

But then again, he was *really* thirsty.

How much harm could one sip of root beer really do?

CHAPTER TWO

Well, one little sip turned into a big, long gulp. Before Darren knew he'd done it, the entire bottle was empty. Almost immediately, Darren could feel the soda churning. His stomach rumbled like a dormant volcano on the verge of waking up. Gas expanded inside him.

CLENCH

His butt had to clench tight to hold it in.

Just keep calm, he told himself. He knew from experience that spazzing out only ended up in explosive results. Maybe if he just kept cool the brewing eruption would subside. He grimaced and clutched his stomach. *I can do this. I can control it.*

"You okay?" Andy asked.

"I'm fine," Darren fibbed. "Just a little carsick from the ride here."

Andy had no idea just how powerful Darren's gas had become. Darren hated hiding his secret from his friend, but it wasn't just *his* secret to share. There was the rest of the Fart Squad to consider, too. None of them wanted to be famous for being able to make superpowered stinks.

"And that's the story of the Buttzville Tar Pit," Professor Paleo said, concluding his lecture. "Any questions?"

Harry Buttz raised his hand. His

designer clothes and haircut advertised how rich and important his family was. "Yeah. When is this dump shutting down again?"

"Shutting down?" Darren asked.

"That's right," Harry said with a smirk. "My dad is already planning to buy the property and turn it into a hangar for his private jet."

Darren figured Harry had to be making a bad joke. The museum was priceless.

"Is it true?" Darren was the first to ask.

"I'm afraid so, Darren," the old curator said sadly. "Attendance isn't what it used to be. I'm not sure how much longer we can stay in business."

Darren glanced around. He hadn't noticed before, but now he saw that the museum looked a little shabby and run-down. Peeling paint and rusty signs needed touching up. Weeds sprouted in the grass and between the paving stones.

"See?" Harry said. "Told you!"

Darren was crushed. What would happen

to all the cool old fossils, not to mention Professor Paleo? And what about all the dinosaur bones that might still be hidden at the bottom of the tar pit? Now they would never be discovered!

"That's enough, Harry," Miss Priscilly said. "Let's just enjoy our trip. Everyone follow me. It's time to go see what Buttzville was like more than a hundred million years ago."

The museum had a large domed auditorium where they showed 3D movies about the age of dinosaurs. Darren and the other kids filed into the theater and took their seats. They *ooh*ed and *aah*ed as the movie started and the sights and sounds of a prehistoric swamp sprang to life all around them. Insects chittered and buzzed in the background as plant-eating dinosaurs fed on palm trees, ferns, and mosses. Winged pterosaurs circled in the sky. Sea serpents splashed in a lagoon.

Ordinarily, Darren would be all eyes and ears, but the half-digested pretzels and root beer churned in his gut, filling his stomach with hot gas. He felt a volcanic *blatt* building inside him, just like he felt right after he'd first eaten those radioactive burritos. This wasn't going to be just some silly little toot. This was going to be a *monster* fart.

And there was no way he could hold it in much longer.

"Excuse me!" Darren jumped to his feet and rushed out of the auditorium. "I need to get some air!"

"Darren . . . ," Ms. Priscilly yelled, but

this time there was no stopping him. He rushed outside, careful not to run too hard and loosen the fart prematurely. The pressure was getting more uncomfortable by the moment. It felt like it was going to be a butt-blazer. He ducked in the decorative ferns around the tar pit, turned his backside toward Buttosaurus, and let 'er rip.

A *blaaatt* louder than a foghorn sounded as a blast of stinky, super-heated gas erupted from Darren's butt. The ferns around him crumbled instantly into ash. The fart was stronger and hotter than any Darren had ever loosed before. His butt burned like he had just pooped hot coals. Gulping, he spun around to inspect the damage, but what he saw was way worse than he'd expected.

The heat of his fart had actually *melted* the tar pit, turning the thick sludge into a percolating pool of gooey black liquid.

Bubbles rose from deep within the pit, and when the bubbles popped they let loose a rancid smell that made Darren's eruption smell like roses by comparison.

Uh-oh, Darren thought. *What have I done?*

CHAPTER THREE

Everybody came rushing out of the museum.

"What was that?" Miss Priscilly said in

alarm. "Did I hear an explosion?"

"What happened?" Professor Paleo asked. "What's that smell?"

Darren wasn't going to admit to farting, let alone to melting the tar pit with his fart.

"I'm not sure," he fudged. "I was just standing here, minding my own business, when the tar pit started bubbling."

"It could be a freak geothermal reaction," Professor Paleo said.

"Sounds right," Stan said. He was the only adult who knew about the Fart Squad, and he knew how important it was to protect the kids' identities. "That must be it."

The Professor peered at the melted tar. "But . . . for it to heat this quickly and to this temperature . . . It's scientifically impossible."

"I don't see another explanation," Stan said.

"That may be, but . . ."

And before Professor Paleo could finish his thought, the tar pit bubbled and belched. The sickening smell increased. Miss Priscilly turned green. She tottered unsteadily on her feet. "Oh my," she moaned right before she fainted.

But the smell wasn't the only thing rising from the pool of melted tar.

"Look out!" Andy pointed at the pit. "There's something stirring in there!"

Everyone gasped and stared in shock as an *actual, living* dinosaur began to climb out of the pit. An enormous head rose from the tar with a roar. This wasn't just a lifeless collection of bones. It was flesh and blood and huge teeth dripping with hot tar and saliva. A giant stepped out of the pit and shook its head and shoulders like a wet dog. Scalding-hot tar splattered everywhere. And then it raised its tail—and Darren was sure he could

see it smile just a moment before it let loose with a fart 150 million years in the making.

"Oh no," Darren muttered. "The Buttosaurus, it's come back to life."

"That's no Buttosaurus," Professor Paleo cried. "Its hindquarters are too muscular. No, I'm afraid this is a Fartasaurus. It's a relative of the Buttosaurus and the most dangerous gas-passing animal that's ever lived!"

Panic broke out as the Fartasaurus used its upper forelimbs to clean itself off. Big yellow eyes looked around curiously.

"Watch out, everyone!" Professor Paleo shouted. He backed away from the pit, only to slip on a puddle of greasy tar. His feet slid out from under him, his head thumped against the pavement, and he knocked himself out cold.

"Professor!" Darren exclaimed, but his cry was drowned out by all the shrieking around him. Pretty much the entire fourth grade ran from the pit, with Harry Buttz shoving past everybody else to lead the retreat.

But not everybody ran. Juan-Carlos, Tina, and Walter hurried over to join Darren. The Fart Squad was together again.

"Whoa, dude!" Juan-Carlos Finkelstein was too stunned to crack one of his usual bad jokes. "That doesn't look like a fossil to me!"

"Evidently this particular saurian was preserved in a state of suspended animation until the congealed asphalt liquefied," said Walter Turnip, whose vocabulary was as big as his bulging midsection. "Or so I am inclined to speculate."

Tina Heiney got straight to the point. She looked like a petite little princess, but in this case, looks were deceiving. "So what are we

going to do about this?"

"I don't know," Darren admitted, but he knew he couldn't just run away like the others. This was his fault. He'd never be able to live with himself if a rampaging dinosaur destroyed Buttzville. "We need to fix this...."

"You bet," Juan-Carlos said. "What's the point of having superpowers if you don't get to save your town from giant monsters once in a while?"

"Indubitably," Walter agreed.

"I suppose," Tina sighed, snapping a picture with her phone.

The Fartasaurus rose up on its powerful hind legs and sniffed the air. It was the size of a two-story building and had to weigh two tons at least. Jagged spines ran down its back and onto its tail. Its stomach grumbled and it licked its lips.

And then without warning, it turned and smashed through the safety rail around the pit. The Fart Squad stared in horror as it stomped across the grounds of the exhibit, crushing benches and educational signs. Its tail swung into a dinosaur skeleton, smashing it to pieces.

Fossilized bones clattered onto the pavement. An immense skull rolled past Darren. He had to leap out of the way

to avoid being crushed. *This dino is dangerous*, Darren thought just as he heard Andy scream, "Darren, man, come on! We have to get out of here!"

But Darren hesitated. He couldn't run

away. He was Fart Squad and Fart Squad never ran from a fight. But how was he going to explain this to Andy?

Fortunately, he didn't have to. "Andy," Stan yelled. "Help me over here. We need to get Miss Priscilly and the professor to safety."

Andy ran to assist the janitor, who slid his lunch pail over to Darren and the others as Andy struggled to lift his teacher to safety. Stan nodded to Darren, before helping Andy carrying the unconscious grown-ups away

SKSSSSS

from the rampaging Fartasaurus. It was up to the Fart Squad alone to deal with the ferocious F. Rex.

Darren scrambled over to the lunch pail. He cracked it open, knowing already what was inside: four cold, radioactive burritos.

They were the product of the Buttzville Elementary School cafeteria. In Buttzville nobody ever dared eat the school's bean-and-meat burrito special. Rather than throw them out, however, the frugal lunch ladies just reheated the burritos in the microwave again and again and again, week after week, year after year,

for decades. Eventually, the beans and meat turned radioactive. So when Darren, Tina, Walter, and Juan-Carlos ate them, they soon discovered that the disgusting leftovers had given them amazing fart-abilities.

And soon after, the Fart Squad was born.

"From great farts come mighty winds," Stan liked to say. He had been the one to teach them to use their new flatu-powers, and he'd been holding on to a stash of "special" burritos ever since, just in case the Fart Squad's talents ever needed to be recharged again. And a rampaging fart monster seemed like just their kind of emergency.

"All right, everybody," Darren said, clapping his hands together. "Time to fuel up!"

But before they could even unwrap the first one, Juan-Carlos screamed, "Watch out!" The four kids barely got out of the

way as the lumbering Fartasaurus smashed
through the museum fence and headed for
downtown Buttzville. Cars and motorcycles

crunched beneath its paws. A billboard advertising a new science-fiction movie smashed, splintered, and fell over. Men, women, and children ran from the berserk monster, which lifted a smelly Dumpster with its powerful jaw before spitting it out in disgust.

"Somebody call Animal Control!" Juan-Carlos said. "That lizard is off the leash!"

Walter watched in awe for a moment before gobbling down his burrito in two swift bites. Tina took a cloth napkin and silverware out of her backpack. She ate hers like she was having high tea with the queen, fingers out and perfect manners. When she was done, she burped. "Okay, that was kinda gross."

Darren's own stomach already felt rumbly enough, so he stuck his burrito into his back pocket for later, just in case.

Juan-Carlos clutched his middle. "Oh, that did the trick all right. I'm cooking with gas again."

"Just keep it clenched, guys," Darren said. "We're going to need everything we've

got to stop that creature!"

Looking north, Darren saw the Fartasaurus heading into the heart of town. Screams, crashes, honking horns, and squealing brakes made it easy to keep track of where it was heading.

"Let's go," Darren said, taking charge. "It's time to fight farts with farts!"

CHAPTER FOUR

Sirens blared as the Buttzville Police Department responded to the emergency. Spinning lights flashed on top of the squad cars, which squealed to a halt in front of the oncoming Fartasaurus. Startled police officers piled out of the cars. Their jaws dropped and their eyes bulged. Buttzville was a fairly quiet little town. Darren guessed that the police had never had to deal with a rampaging dinosaur before.

"Halt!" a policeman shouted through a bullhorn. "Sit! Stay! Play dead!"

The Fartasaurus ignored the commands. Instead it turned around and lifted its tail. A thunderous blast sent the cops flying backward, head over heels. A disgusting smell, like a truckload of spoiled eggs, overpowered the police. They staggered to their feet, choking and gagging for air. People ran past, screaming, crying, knocking policemen and policewomen over to get away.

Cars crashed, glass shattered, and broken fire hydrants sprayed water into the air. It was total chaos.

"Retreat!" the lead officer shouted. "Clear out this area and get all these civilians away from here. We need backup for this!"

The cops cleared the area and then jumped in their cars and sped away from the angry Fartasaurus.

"Things are getting out of control," Darren said. "We need to take down that dinosaur, fast!"

"What's the plan?" Tina asked.

Good question, Darren thought. "Try to herd it back into the pit? Using our powers?"

"Works for me," Juan-Carlos said. "Let's go kick some stinky dinosaur butt!"

The Fart Squad changed into costume and leaped into action. Walter's fart-power was that he got so gassy he could turn into a human helium balloon. He jumped up and down a few times to make sure that he was fully inflated and then he let go of the rail he was holding and lifted off into the sky.

He propelled himself with jets of passed gas toward the Fartasaurus. He usually wore a crash helmet when flying, just in case, but he hadn't brought one along on the field trip. He was a pretty good ways up in the air before he realized that a rough landing was really going to hurt.

"I must say," he called out, "I do believe I'm actually becoming more proficient at my aerial maneuvers!"

"Just watch where you're flying!" Darren shouted back at him.

Startled by the airborne intruder, the creature let out an ear-splitting squawk and swatted at Walter with its clawed forelimbs. But Walter had been training long and hard with their scent-sei Stan and the flying fourth-grader swooped away from the monster's reach.

"You're not as fast as you think!" he hollered. "Return to the primeval abyss whence you came! You're supposed to be extinct!"

The Fartasaurus spun at Walter like a toddler with jam on his hands trying to chase away a bee.

While the Fartasaurus was distracted by Walter, Tina and Juan-Carlos crept closer. Juan-Carlos darted ahead first. His fart power was the time bomb. He could leave behind stink that wouldn't be smelt until he was well out of range. He may have dealt it but Juan-Carlos never smelt it! So Juan-Carlos left a series of stink bombs in the dinosaur's path. They went off one by one as the Fartasaurus stomped down the middle of

Main Street. The rapid-fire blasts of nasty smells would have knocked out most normal creatures, but the giant monster just sniffed the air and smiled.

"Seriously?" Juan-Carlos asked in disbelief. "I think he actually likes the smell of farts."

Meanwhile, Tina appeared to be minding her own business, but Darren knew better. Tina's farts were silent but deadly. With their scent-sei's help, she'd learned how to control herself so that you'd never know from looking her in the face that she was squeezing one out. And her gas was the most powerful of all; one whiff usually knocked a normal person out cold. Tina zeroed in on the Fartasaurus. She looked so innocent and harmless. Darren had no idea that she'd even farted until he saw her rush around a corner to safety as if she expected the creature to come crashing down on her.

The Fartasaurus took a deep breath and then wrinkled its snout. It swayed atop its enormous legs. Yellow eyes rolled in their sockets. It rubbed them and yawned.

Yes! Darren thought. *Way to go, Tina!*

But the monster shook its head to clear the fog from its brain. It stopped swaying and regained its balance. Its yawn turned into a ferocious roar. Even Tina's farts weren't strong enough to knock it out. The Fartasaurus raised its tail—and sent a gale-force fart at the squad. Tina and Darren

tumbled backward down the street from the force of the fart alone. A horrible stench, even more pungent than their own atomic farts, washed over the kids. Darren was suddenly very grateful for his superpowers. If he wasn't fart-o-fied, as Scent-sei Stan called their immunity to all things stinky, Darren was sure he'd be out for the count and about to be dinosaur food.

Even still, Fartasaurus Rex outgassed the Fart Squad.

Unless Darren could turn things around.

CHAPTER FIVE

During the week, the Buttzville Farmer's Market occupied the park in the center of town. Lining the paths were stalls that sold everything from fruits and vegetables to homemade cookies and cupcakes. Water sprayed from a marble fountain in the middle of the square. On an ordinary weekday, the market would be packed with shoppers squeezing the melons and sniffing the asparagus, but today people were running and screaming. Because, of course, a giant farting prehistoric monster

was lumbering toward them.

The Fartasaurus roared first before it turned, lifted its tail, and let out a fart so rancid it made the air shimmy as it traveled. Darren watched, horrified, as Roger the mailman made the mistake of turning

toward the sound as he was running away. He took a single whiff and fell to the ground. *This must be how the Fartasaurus hunts,*

Darren thought. *It stuns its prey with its powerful farts.* Darren was sure that Roger was as good as lunch—unless Darren did something daring. Running as fast as he could, he dodged the Fartasaurus's swinging tail and dashed between the monster's mammoth legs. It was up to him now to stop the beast. Fortunately, all this excitement

had churned up his already upset stomach; his butt was ready to erupt again.

"Here goes nothing," he said. "Ready, aim . . . fart!"

The fiery blast burned on its way out. He felt like he was sitting on a flame thrower, but the Fartasaurus seemed unfazed. It peered down at its chest with a puzzled expression. The creature just bulled past Darren right into the center fountain. The water

washed the last of the gooey black gunk from its body. Its green scales glistened in the sunlight. The creature shook itself like a dog again. It would have been cute—if it wasn't a giant, man-eating monster.

The Fartasaurus seemed to notice Darren staring at it, and a moment later it remembered it was mad. The fart monster crashed through the marble bowl of the fountain and came at Darren. It had Darren pinned against a wall of toppled vegetable stands. There was nowhere to run. There was no

escape. Slobber dripped
from the Fartasaurus's
jaws. It eagerly
licked its chops.
Its stomach
growled omi-
nously.

Uh-oh,   Darren
thought. *Maybe I didn't quite think this
through. . . .*

The Fartasaurus opened its jaws wide.
Its breath was almost as bad as the smell
coming from the other end of its digestive
system. Darren flinched and braced himself
for the end. The dinosaur lunged forward,
ready to chomp, bearing a row of huge flat
teeth. . . .

And it darted right past Darren and
started gobbling up the vegetables behind
him instead.

"Huh?"

Scrambling out of the way, Darren stared in confusion as the "ferocious" monster chomped down on bushels of defenseless cabbages, broccoli, and Brussels sprouts, completely ignoring the tender human morsel nearby. Its tail wagged happily as it feasted on the veggies. Darren was puzzled at first, until he took another look at the creature's mouth. Unlike the razor-sharp fangs on the demolished skeleton back at the museum, the Fartasaurus's teeth were square and stumpy.

"It's not a predator at all," Darren realized. "It's a plant-eater!"

CHAPTER SIX

The rest of the Fart Squad caught up with Darren. Juan-Carlos and Tina tugged on his arms, trying to drag him away from the market and the hungry Fartasaurus.

"Come on," Juan-Carlos said. "We need to make tracks before that monster finishes its salad. We could be the next item on the menu!"

"Wait," Darren said. "I think we've had this all wrong. It's not dangerous at all, just lost and confused ... and very, very hungry."

"That's not what they said at the museum," Tina said. "The Professor said it was a relative of the Buttosaurus and that the Buttosaurus was a ferocious predator."

"They must have put the wrong skull on that skeleton," Darren guessed, "and mixed up two different dinosaurs." Scientists had made similar mistakes before, he knew, when putting fossils together like jigsaw puzzles. He remembered noticing that the fossil's skull was shaped differently from the living dinosaur's. "This one is harm-less!"

"Well, I wouldn't go that far," Tina said. Her nose wrinkled above her face mask. "Look at how it's gobbling down all that cabbage, broccoli, and sprouts. No wonder it's a *Fart*asaurus!"

She had a point. The creature seemed to have a taste for gas-producing veggies.

"So now what?" Juan-Carlos asked. "We're just going to let it graze—like a prehistoric cow?"

"Maybe."

Darren didn't see any point in fighting the Fartasaurus now that they knew it didn't want to eat people. It occurred to him that most of the damage so far had actually been caused by people panicking, not by the Fartasaurus itself. Perhaps all they needed to do was guide the dinosaur back to the museum, where it could be studied and taken care of by Professor Paleo. He remembered what he had told Andy before, about how great it would be to see an actual living, breathing dinosaur. He had gotten his wish all right.

"We need to save this animal, not stop it!"

"That could be harder than it sounds." Tina glanced down at her smartphone. "There's an emergency alert on the internet. A police SWAT team is on its way and they're not messing around. They're bringing rocket launchers and grenades and who knows what else."

"Oh no!" Darren exclaimed. "They don't need to do that!"

He was horrified by the idea of the police

launching a full-scale attack on the harmless dinosaur. He looked over at the Fartasaurus, who was still happily munching on the veggies, wagging its tail. An enormous burp slipped from its snout as it moved from one vegetable stall to the next. It really was kinda cute, Darren realized, now that he knew it wasn't going to eat anybody.

"Maybe we can explain," he said.

"Yeah, right," Juan-Carlos scoffed. "Who's going to pay attention to a couple of kids when there's a scary-looking prehistoric creature on the loose? If it looks like a monster and stomps like a monster, they're going to treat it like a monster! It's dino-profiling, I tell you!"

Darren had seen enough monster movies to know that Juan-Carlos had a point. The army always fought the rampaging beast in the end. No way was anyone going to listen

to them while the runaway dinosaur was still running amok.

"We need to get the Fartasaurus back to the museum," he decided. "If it's back where it belongs and not stomping through town,

people might calm down long enough to figure out that it's just a big vegetarian after all."

"But the SWAT team is already on its way," Tina said. "We're running out of time."

A plan began to form in Darren's head. "That's where you and Juan-Carlos come in. I need you to slow down the police while Walter and I lure the F. Rex back to the museum. Do you think you can do that?"

Tina smirked. "Just watch us."

"You bet," Juan-Carlos agreed. "'Distracting' is my middle name."

"I thought that was 'Unfunny,'" Tina said.

"Everybody's a critic."

Walter swooped lower to join in the conversation. "What about yours truly?" he inquired. "How exactly do you intend to entice yonder herbivore back to its formerly antediluvian stomping grounds? And where precisely do I fit into your stratagem?"

Darren spotted a stall of fresh vegetables that the Fartasaurus hadn't gotten to yet. A canvas banner stretched above the stand. He grinned at Walter.

"How much cabbage can you lift?"

CHAPTER SEVEN

Tina and Juan-Carlos took off on their mission. Tina thought it felt strange going into action without the other half of the Squad beside them, but sometimes teamwork meant splitting up and trusting your friends.

"You sure you know what to do?" she grilled Juan-Carlos. "No joking?"

"Just watch! I'm going to make like the

wind." He snickered. "Make wind, get it?"

Tina rolled her eyes. "Cool the comedy and get going."

He hurried away, leaving Tina behind. She could hear the sirens from blocks away. She ran toward the commotion, hoping she could get to the SWAT team before it got to the defenseless Fartasaurus.

The strike team was zooming down Main Street like a parade. Flashing red lights spun on top of an entire fleet of police cars and vans. Motorcycles roared alongside the larger vehicles. There was even an armored tank rolling down the street at the front of the caravan.

Where the heck did that come from? Tina wondered. *Fort Buttz?*

She gulped and checked to make sure her mask was in place. She couldn't believe she was actually doing this—and for a stinky dinosaur no less. Still, she didn't want an innocent animal to end up extinct again. The Fartasaurus was one of a kind.

Working up her nerve, she rushed into the street right in front of the oncoming vehicles, which slammed on their brakes at the sight of the little girl. The top of the tank flipped open and a police commander climbed out. He had on black body armor and a helmet. His name, SPANK, was printed in block letters on his chest. She guessed he was the leader of the SWAT team.

"You shouldn't be here, little lady," he said. "It's not safe!"

"I ran away from the monster!" she sobbed, pretending to be scared. She sniffled and wiped fake tears from her eyes. She

pointed away from the market toward the other side of town. "It's heading that way! Toward my school!"

"Are you sure about that?" He took off his helmet to reveal a puzzled expression. "That's not what we—"

A *blaatt* like a sonic boom came from a nearby side street, maybe a block away. A disgusting odor wafted from the same direction.

Tina smirked behind her face mask. For once, Juan-Carlos's timing was perfect.

"You see? You smell that? It's over there!"

Officer Spank's nose wrinkled and he made a face. "Hmm. That does smell like our target. . . ."

Another stink bomb went off somewhere to the east, on the other side of the street, and then a few blocks behind the troops. Rude noises and smells started popping up in every direction, just out of sight. Juan-Carlos was clearly covering a lot of ground.

"What in the world?" Spank looked around in confusion. "I thought there was only one monster?"

A motorcycle trooper called out to the police commander. "Which way are we going?"

"Hang on a sec!" Spank said, flustered. "Let me think. . . ."

Tina didn't give him a chance. Nobody heard a thing, but Spank suddenly gagged and placed a hand over his mouth. His eyes rolled backward until only the whites could be seen and he collapsed limply onto the pavement. He was out cold.

"Commander!" The other cops rushed forward. "What happened to him?"

Tina shrugged innocently. "I'm sure I have no idea."

Baffled troopers looked at one another, unsure who was in charge now, or which way the Fartasaurus was heading. Noisy stink bombs kept going off all around, in every direction except the right one.

That should slow things down, Tina thought. *But did we buy Darren and Walter enough time to get the F. Rex to safety?*

CHAPTER EIGHT

"**H**urry! It's gaining on you!"

Darren shouted up at Walter, who was cruising through the sky like a blimp. Bushels of cabbage, suspended in a sling made from a "borrowed" banner, weighed Walter down. He was barely managing to keep ahead of the hungry Fartasaurus chasing after him. Drool poured from the dinosaur's jaws. Its wide yellow eyes were fixed on the lucky veggies that slipped out.

"Rest assured that I am sufficiently aware

of that fact," Walter said, straining to stay aloft. "I am proceeding as expeditiously as possible, under the circumstances!"

"Stop talking. Save the air for your butt!" Darren called back.

He ran ahead of Walter, leading the way past deserted shopping centers, gas stations, and used-car lots. They had successfully lured the F. Rex away from the market square, but the museum was still a block away. Darren heard police sirens in the distance and wondered how much time they had left to get the dinosaur to safety.

He knew he could count on Tina and Juan-Carlos to throw some smelly obstacles in the SWAT team's path, but farts only went so far.

Even super ones.

The Fartasaurus squawked in frustration. It snapped at Walter, who was now barely out of reach. It stomped down the middle of the street on its hind legs, moving a lot more quickly than Darren expected. Its tail smashed cars and lampposts as it ran. It had worked up quite an appetite over the last 150 million years!

"Keep going!" Darren shouted, cheering Walter on. "You're almost there!"

"So near and yet so far," Walter moaned. "My formidable flatulence is all but exhausted!"

Dragged down by the weight of all those cabbages, Walter hovered dangerously close to the frantic Fartasaurus. The museum was just around the corner. Darren knew now that the F. Rex didn't actually want to eat Walter, but still, it was dangerous. The last thing Walter needed was to get dragged down to earth by a two-ton lizard that didn't know its own strength. A final desperate toot propelled Walter out of harm's way just in time. He was falling more than he was flying at this point. One burrito hadn't been enough.

"Dump the veggies!" Darren yelled. "Save yourself!"

"Negative!" Walter flapped his arms to try to stay in the air. "I can still achieve our objective. . . ."

Darren ran as fast as he could to keep up. He darted through the broken fence surrounding the museum grounds.

"Watch out for the tar pit!" Darren warned.

For a second, it really looked like Walter
was going to splash down into the gooey pool
of liquid asphalt, but he made it just past the
pit before crash landing on the grassy lawn.
A hefty heap of cabbages squashed beneath
him to cushion his landing.

"Oomph!" Walter grunted. "I do believe
I need to work on my landing technique. Or
perhaps invest in a para-
chute. . . ."

"Later!" Darren
helped Walter to
his feet. The Fart-
asaurus leaped over
the sticky tar pit and
landed on the grounds
between the pit and
the museum build-
ing. Darren and
Walter darted

away, hiding behind a row of shrubs, but the hungry dinosaur was only interested in the pile of smushed cabbages. As it gobbled down the gas-producing veggies, a monstrous fart snuck out from beneath its tail.

"A unique defense mechanism," Walter speculated, "intended to stun predators."

"That sounds about right," Darren said. Evolution had given the Fartasaurus a very stinky way to protect itself. "That smell would kill the appetite of most meat-eaters!"

Darren was breathing hard after running back and forth across town. Even his excess energy had its limit and he was nearing his. He appreciated the time-out while the F. Rex pigged out on cabbage, but he knew the veggies weren't going to occupy the restless creature for long. The Fartasaurus was bound to go stomping off again unless he found a way to keep it here, safely out of trouble.

Good thing he knew just what to do.

Leaving Walter hiding behind a leafy palm tree, Darren sprinted into the empty auditorium, where the 3D simulation of the

Age of Dinosaurs was still playing. A door marked AUTHORIZED PERSONNEL ONLY led to the theater's control room, which had been abandoned in the panic. Darren turned up the volume on the show. Prehistoric bugs and lizards made a tremendous racket, which sounded just like Buttzville had . . . 150 million years ago.

Or so Darren hoped.

Darren ran back into the auditorium while sirens blared outside. The police would be here any minute. Time was running out for the innocent Fartasaurus. There was only one thing to do. He pulled the spare burrito from his back pocket and tore open the foil wrapping. The recycled cafeteria fare was cold, soggy, and unappetizing, but this was an emergency. He crammed the burrito into his mouth whole. As usual, it was super-spicy, with a peculiar flavor he could never quite place. Gushy beans and atomic salsa tingled his tongue and oozed down his throat, reigniting the rumbling volcano in his gut. He clenched his teeth to keep from barfing it up.

It was like throwing gasoline on hot coals. All at once, Darren felt another eruption coming. He heard the homesick dinosaur squawking mournfully outside, trying to get in. Giant claws scratched loudly at the too-small door. He aimed his butt at the theater door.

"Fire in the hole!" Darren shouted.

The explosive blast scorched the rear of Darren's jeans and blew a hole in the wall big enough for a twenty-foot-tall dinosaur to pass through. He ducked out of the way as the Fartasaurus charged into the auditorium. It screeched happily to find itself back home in a prehistoric swamp—or at least a convincing imitation of one. Its tail wagged back and forth.

Darren grinned.

The Fartasaurus was back where it belonged—sort of.

CHAPTER NINE

Weeks later, the fourth grade returned to the exhibit, which was now called the Buttzville Prehistoric Tar Pit & Dinosaur Habitat. It was a lot more crowded than before. Wide-eyed tourists from all over lined up for hours to see the world's only living Fartasaurus, who was now grazing happily in its own specially designed habitat, complete with genuine palm trees, ferns, fresh water, and generous amounts of fresh veggies. Now that the museum was a success again, it could afford to buy the friendly

dinosaur all the cabbage, broccoli, and Brussels sprouts it could eat. Filter masks came with your ticket, just in case the atmosphere got a little too pungent. The crowd cheered and clapped as the F. Rex lifted its tail and proved once again that, yep, it was a Fartasaurus all right.

Professor Paleo, now wearing a gas mask as well as a pith helmet, greeted another batch of sightseers.

"So much for turning this place into an airplane hangar," Darren said to his friends. "Look at all these people!"

The Fartasaurus had saved the museum, after the Fart Squad had saved the dinosaur. There had been a few tense moments when the SWAT team finally reached the museum, but once they saw that the "dangerous" creature was under control and not out to eat anybody, everyone had calmed

down. Nobody wanted to hurt a harmless plant-eater who was happy to stay where it was.

Everything had turned out okay, except maybe for the Buttz family, who would have to stow their private jet elsewhere. Darren noticed Harry scowling in the background.

A contest was being held to name the F. Rex. "Thunder" was in first place ... and not because of its heavy footsteps.

"I think we should make it an honorary member of the Fart Squad," Tina whispered. "Or maybe our official team mascot."

"Works for me," Darren said.

He had always loved dinosaurs.

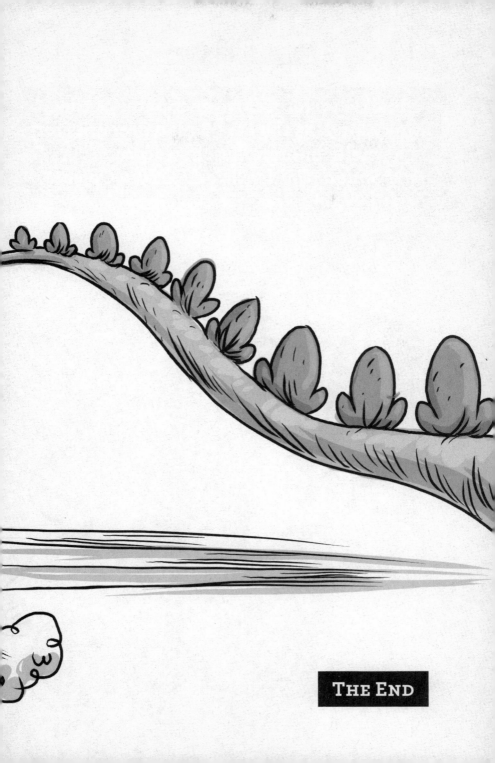

THE END

Buckle up for a close encounter of the stinky kind, as the Fart Squad prepares for a smelly interstellar showdown in . . . *Fart Squad: Unidentified Farting Objects.*